D0567449

The MISADVENTURES of Phillip Isaac Penn

PIP GOES TO CAMP

Donna L. Peterson

BONNEVILLE BOOKS
AN IMPRINT OF CEDAR FORT, INC.
SPRINGVILLE, UTAH

This is a work of fiction. The characters, names, incidents, places, and dialogue are products of the author's imagination and are not to be construed as real.

ISBN 13: 978-1-4621-1077-3

Published by Bonneville Books, an imprint of Cedar Fort, Inc.
2373 W. 700 S., Springville, UT 84663
Distributed by Cedar Fort, Inc., www.cedarfort.com

LIBRARY OF CONGRESS CATALOGING-IN-PUBLICATION DATA
Peterson, Donna (Donna Lee), 1956- author.
Pip goes to camp / Donna L. Peterson.
pages cm. -- (Misadventures of Phillip Isaac Penn)
Summary: Pip's parents pack him off to summer camp where he runs into several colorful characters as he endures his eight days of "torture."
ISBN 978-1-4621-1077-3 (alk. paper)
[1. Camps--Fiction. 2. Interpersonal relations--Fiction. 3. Ability--Fiction. 4. Conduct of life--Fiction.] I. Title. II. Series: Peterson, Donna (Donna Lee), 1956-. Misadventures of Phillip Isaac Penn.

PZ7.P443338Pip 2012
[Fic]--dc23

2012016331

Illustrations by Rachel Sharp
Cover design by Danie Romrell
Cover design © 2012 by Lyle Mortimer
Edited and typeset by Melissa J. Caldwell

Printed in the United States of America

10 9 8 7 6 5 4 3 2 1

Printed on acid-free paper

This is dedicated to my family and the families I grew up with who share my most precious childhood memories: the Norgords, Nielsens, Washkos, Mills, and Works. With warm wishes to a special young lady named Kyleigh Rose. And to all children everywhere, who now know that they aren't alone when it comes to thinking, "It just isn't easy being a kid."

Contents

Contents

1

Pip Goes to Camp

Hi. I'm Phillip Isaac Penn, but everyone calls me Pip. Sometimes my ears hurt from hearing my own name. Wherever I go, I can always hear somebody shouting, "Pip!"

Yep, today I started out feeling real happy because it was the last day of school. Nothing is better than summer vacation!

Everything was okay until my dad hollered, "Pip!" Then he told me he had some "great news."

"What is it?" I wanted to know. "Are we going to Disneyland or Disney World?"

"Nope." He shook his head. "Maybe next year . . ."

"Oh." I was disappointed, but I took another guess. "Are we going to camp someplace where there's a lake and we can go fishing?"

My dad smiled real funny, kind of like I was getting close to guessing his "great news." That's when he held up a handful of folded pictures and told me, "You're headed for eight fun-filled days of summer camp."

"What do you mean?" I wanted to know, hoping it wasn't what I thought it was going to be.

He laid the folded pictures (he called them *brochures*) on top of the kitchen table and read about all the *exciting activities* he thought I'd enjoy. But they didn't sound that fun to me. Nope! It just sounded like more school, and even kind of like a prison.

"I don't want to waste part of my summer going to some dumb ol' camp!" I told him.

He just kept telling me how I'd "have so many great experiences," and it would be "good for me." He even told me that it would help me to "mature."

After he walked away and left me with all of those brochures to look at, I got a dictionary and looked up the word "m-u-c-h-e-r." It wasn't even in there.

When my dad came back into the kitchen, I asked him what "mucher" means.

He told me, "The word is *mature*, and it means to grow up." Then he patted me on my head and said, "You can't be a kid forever, Pip."

Well, I'd sure rather be a kid than a grown-up who gets headaches all the time from paying bills. Yeah, I'm sure in no hurry to be "mature."

My morning didn't get any better when

my big sister, K.D., came into the room with a mean smile on her face. "Looks like you just found out you're going off to camp. That means I'll have a real vacation for once since I won't have you around pestering me!"

"How come *you* don't have to go to camp?" I wanted to know.

"I guess Mom and Dad just like me better, and they don't mind having me around." She smiled real big. "And maybe they're looking forward to having you gone as much as I'm looking forward to it."

Boy, was I getting more and more angry. She always thinks she's so great and that everyone likes her better than me. But I did sort of wonder if maybe it was true. What if they *did* like my sister better than me? And what if they *were* happy that I'd be gone?

I stomped off to my room, hoping to just be alone for a while. Only I couldn't even be alone in my own room because my mom was there. She was folding up shirts and putting them into my suitcase, which was already stuffed full of clothes.

"Pip!" she hollered as she crammed in a few more pairs of socks. "Come help me pack for your vacation!"

"Gee, Mom, you sure are in a big hurry to get rid of me."

"Don't be so silly, Pip." She reached over and ruffled up my hair. "It's only for eight days. But you'll need to get ready right away because camp starts tomorrow afternoon."

"What?" I shouted. I couldn't believe it. I didn't even have a chance to enjoy a whole day of summer vacation before I had to go off to prison—I mean camp. My mom told me that they'd already paid for it, so I had to "go and give it a try." Nope! They didn't even care if I wanted to go or not.

I was so mad that I punched the door on my way out.

"Watch your temper, young man!" my mom yelled after me.

The next morning, my dad drove up behind a bus parked beside a sign that said, "Community Center Summer Camp."

Yeah, I sure felt like a criminal as they pushed me toward that big ol' bus.

My dad gave me a pat on the back and told me I'd be "making memories and new friends." My mom wiped a tear off her cheek, so I thought maybe she might miss me after all. Then she gave me a quick hug and told me to remember to change my underwear every day.

Yeah, I looked around real quick, just to make sure nobody heard that. Gee, they'd be laughing at me all week if they'd heard my mom say that crazy thing.

After the bus pulled away, I tried not to cry. I just dug into my backpack and grabbed my MP3 player. I jammed the ear buds in and turned my music up full blast, then I looked around to see who else was being sent off to prison—uh . . . camp.

That's when I saw one of my worst enemies from school: Cheater Chaz. He looked right at me with real tough eyes.

Even though I couldn't hear him, I saw him mouth the words, "Oh, no! Not you!"

Yep, I sure wished I wasn't on that ol' bus. And I knew I'd really be glad when those eight days of summer camp were over. It's just not easy being a kid.

2

Bunking with Whiner Winston

We finally got to that dumb ol' summer camp. It sure was the rottenest, longest ride ever. I couldn't wait to get off that darn bus.

Just as I stepped off the bus, my ears were blasted with a real loud whistle. I thought I'd never hear again.

Some guy was blowing that stinking whistle until his cheeks turned all red, and then he shouted, "All right, get into a line!" He blew it again. His cheeks looked like two gigantic red balloons. "I said get into line! You have to line up so you can find out which cabin you're staying in and your room numbers. You'll also need to get your list of scheduled activities . . . and, of course, the rules."

I felt like he was looking right at me when he added, "These rules must be obeyed at all times!" Then he told us his name was Counselor Conrad, the boys' camp counselor.

I looked over at Cheater Chaz, and he made a fist at me.

Boy, did I feel a whole lot better when our camp counselor told me that my roommate was someone named Winston and not that stinking Cheater Chaz. Okay, maybe Winston was kind of a different-sounding name, but at least he looked sort of nice.

Once we got to our cabins, it sure didn't take me long to find out that Winston was a great, big ol' whiner. Yeah, maybe his name should've been Whiner Winston.

"Hey, Pip," he moaned, "I need to sleep on the bottom bunk on account of I get nose bleeds if I'm too high up."

Then he started to complain about everything else. He said the mattress was too hard, and the water didn't get hot enough, and when we went to dinner, he said the food wasn't as good as his mom made things.

I guess he thought we were supposed to be staying at a fancy hotel, or something. Gee, I didn't even want to stay in a cabin. I was really hoping we were going to stay in a tent. Then we'd really be camping. This didn't even seem like a real camp, since there were beds and showers.

The next morning, my eyes burned as if red ants were crawling on the inside of them. I hardly got to sleep all night. Ol' Whiner

Winston was below me, blubbering and bawling the whole time. It sure was a good thing he didn't sleep on top, or I would have drowned down below him.

When that darn whistle blew, we all lined up for breakfast. Winston just covered his ears and complained about how early he had to get up just to eat some food that wasn't going to taste good anyway.

Of course we had to sit next to our *bunk buddies*, as they called them, and I couldn't escape that big ol' whiner.

"The eggs are too cold," he complained, "and the pancakes are like rubber."

I tried to ignore him, but he just wouldn't stop. I didn't know which was worse: his mosquito-sounding whine or that dang whistle that kept blowing.

"My mom would never make sausage this greasy," he moaned. "I just don't know how

I can stand it here another minute."

"Hey," I said, "can't you just stop your stinkin' whining?"

Whiner Winston's eyes filled with tears. "Now you're being mean to me too!" he cried.

"What's going on here?" Counselor Conrad wanted to know. Then he looked right at me. "What have you done, young man?"

Before I could even answer him, the rotten whiner cried out, "He's being mean to me!"

"We don't tolerate bullies around here!" Counselor Conrad shouted in my ear. "So don't let me catch you picking on your bunk buddy again!"

Boy, was I mad. I couldn't help it if I was just sick and tired of listening to that big ol', whining crybaby. I'd like to see how our camp counselor would have liked being stuck with Whiner Winston all day.

After breakfast we all had to meet on the

lawn to play some different games. That's when I met up with a bunch of other kids I didn't think I'd like much. One of them was a bossy kid named Billy, and another was a show-off named Shad.

When our camp counselor wasn't telling us what to do, that bossy kid was trying to take his place. "No! No! No! You don't throw the ball that way!" he yelled at me. "Do it this way!"

Then Show-Off Shad grabbed the ball and spun it on his head. "Watch me!" he shouted.

I thought he was funny the first time, but after that, he started doing the same stunts over and over again. Yeah, it sure looked goofy.

We'd been so busy playing those dumb games that I didn't even notice that Whiner Winston had stopped whining. Then I looked around and saw why I hadn't heard him. He wasn't there.

I thought maybe he'd gone back to our cabin, so I ran back to take a look. Nope, he wasn't in the cabin or anywhere else I looked. I actually started to get worried. Not that I missed that stinking whiner, but I still didn't want him lost in the forest getting eaten by some ol' bear, or something.

When it was time to eat lunch, Counselor Conrad made us line up again so he could take roll call. That's when he noticed that Whiner Winston was missing.

"Hey, Pip," he said as he looked at me with those squinty eyes. "What happened to your bunk buddy, Winston?"

"How would I know?" I asked. I wanted to add, "I'm not his babysitter," but he already wasn't happy with the answer I'd given him, so I just zipped my lip.

"Listen here, Pip," he hissed, "you're skating on thin ice as it is, so you'd better not give me that kind of smart-aleck response."

I thought his words were kind of strange because it was summer and there sure wasn't any ice around anywhere. Plus he was talking about another kid named Alec who I didn't even know. But I guess he must've been pretty smart.

"Besides," he added, "you didn't seem to like your bunk buddy much, so let's hope he's okay." Then he put his nose right next to mine. "You better help me find him if you know what's good for you!"

Our camp counselor made up some kind of *search party*, and we wasted our entire lunchtime looking all through the camp for Whiner Winston.

When I was looking around the place they called the *mess hall*, I smelled our lunch waiting for us. My stomach growled. At first I thought it was a big ol' bear, so I jumped next to a barrel to hide.

That's when I heard this loud sniffling noise coming from inside the barrel. I noticed that the lid wasn't all the way on top of it, so I peeked inside. Yep, there was Whiner Winston, curled up inside, having himself another big cry.

"Hey, kid," I said, trying to sound nice. "Why don't you get out of there so we can all get something to eat? It's past lunchtime, and I'm almost starved to death."

"I don't want to." He sniffed. "They never make anything good anyway."

"Come on!" I shouted. "Some of us are hungry, even if you're not."

"You can't make me do what I don't wanna do!" he shouted back at me.

That was it. I'd had enough. I reached in to pull that rotten whiner out, but the barrel tipped over, and that kid went rolling down the hill, barrel and all.

"H-E-L-P!" he screamed.

Counselor Conrad came from out of nowhere and ran down the hill after that ol' barrel. We all watched as it crashed with a big bang against a gigantic log.

When Whiner Winston crawled out of the barrel, sticks were in his hair, and muddy tears ran down his big, dirty cheeks.

He looked so funny that I just laughed.

That kid just gave me a real mean look, then pointed right at me and yelled, "Pip pushed me!"

"Pip!" Counselor Conrad hollered. "I told you we don't tolerate bullies around here. If that's true and you really did push him down that hill, then you'll have to go home."

I was so excited to finally get some good news. But a few seconds later, the camp cook came running out from the mess hall with her apron flapping.

"Wait!" she shouted out. "I saw the entire incident from the kitchen window. That young man standing next to you," she said, pointing to me, "he was only trying to help that other boy out of the barrel. I don't think he meant for the barrel to take off like it did."

Well, the camp counselor decided to send Winston home instead of me, since the big ol' whiner kept saying he just wanted to go home, and he wouldn't stop crying.

I guess I could have been nicer to Whiner Winston, even though he did complain a lot. He was probably just homesick, sort of like I was feeling.

Yeah, it was kind of funny watching him take off, hollering, inside that barrel. But I guess I shouldn't have laughed at him, because he could've gotten hurt.

It's just not that easy being a kid. And it

sure wasn't much fun being sent off to some dumb ol' camp when I wanted to be at home enjoying my summer vacation.

3

Canoeing with Joker Joey

When I got to roll call the next morning, our camp counselor told us that we'd be getting a new kid to take Winston's place. I guess this kid had been on something called a *waiting list*, so his parents had to drive him up that afternoon. Yep, he was supposed to be my new bunk buddy. I just hoped real hard that he wasn't going to be another big ol' crybaby.

After I got out of craft class, I met the new kid, Joey. When I reached out to shake his hand like we were supposed to do, I felt a jolt shoot clear to my elbow.

"Hey!" I yelled as I jumped back.

He got a big ol' grin, like it was the funniest thing he'd ever seen. "I guess you're shocked to meet me?" He laughed. "My name is Joey."

Just then Counselor Conrad came over to give him the camp schedule and that darn list of camp rules. That stinking joker stuck the metal hand buzzer in his pocket, and then he winked at me, sort of like we were sharing a great big secret.

Yeah, I knew I was going to have problems with that new kid, Joker Joey. I just wished camp would hurry up and be over.

When we went back to our cabin to clean up before dinner, I showed him our bunks. "I'm sleeping on the top bunk," I told him.

"That's real good of you to let me know where you'll be sleeping." He laughed again.

I didn't see what was so funny about showing him where I was sleeping, but it made me kind of nervous the way he kept laughing.

While we ate our dinner at the mess hall, Joker Joey was sneaking pepper into the other kids' food. Then he elbowed me and said, "This is another one of our little secrets, right?"

I just nodded, trying real hard to mind my own business.

But it sure did seem kind of mean when he poured salt into the sugar bowl. Yep, I felt kind of bad for that shy girl named Shannon. She thought she was stirring sugar into her cocoa, and it turned out to be mostly salt.

Shy Shannon turned bright red, and the cocoa shot straight out of her mouth like some kind of geyser.

Oh yeah, that rotten joker laughed so hard that he nearly choked on his french fries.

That gave me an idea. Yep, that ol' joker

needed to have someone teach him a lesson. So when he wasn't looking I took a spoonful of sugar from a different sugar bowl (so I knew it was really sugar), and I tossed it over that joker's fries.

I was just thinking how smart I was for coming up with such a great idea—maybe even as smart as that Alec kid everyone is always talking about. Yep, my eyes were on him the whole time as he picked up about five fries at once and then opened up his big mouth to gulp them down. That's when I heard that darn whistle blow right into my ears.

"Don't eat those fries, young man!" our counselor shouted. "I just saw your bunk buddy"—he looked down at me—"tampering with your food!"

"What?" Joker Joey stared at me real hard. "Pip, how could you?"

That shy girl told the camp counselor that

I must have been the one who had added salt into the sugar bowl, and how her cocoa had been ruined.

"Listen here, Pip," Counselor Conrad said with his nose right next to mine. "Don't let me catch you pulling even one more of your pranks, or your parents will need to come and pick you up!"

When I started to smile, he added, "You and I both know that your parents will not be happy about this, since there are no refunds! I'm quite certain that you will be grounded for the rest of your summer. At least, that's what I'll suggest they do."

Well, that sure took the smile from my face. "Yes sir," I said in my nicest voice.

"Oh, and Pip," he said through his teeth, "tomorrow morning, first thing after break-fast, you owe me thirty push-ups and ten laps around the field."

As soon as our camp counselor was gone, that joker gave me two thumbs up. "Good one, Pip! You're a quick learner. But next time, don't use me as one of your guinea pigs. That'll cost you!" He got a big ol' smile and walked away.

After that warning, I knew I was in for it. I tried real hard to always watch what that joker was doing, just in case he was up to one of his tricks. It was almost worse waiting for him to pay me back. I never knew when Joker Joey would strike again.

When we got back to our cabin, I pulled off my blanket and looked under my pillow before getting into bed. I was sure that a frog or snake was going to be hiding there somewhere. Then I slept with one eye open and just waited for him to try something in the middle of the night.

Yeah, I was nearly asleep when I heard the toilet flush. I sat up straight.

Joker Joey laughed real loud.

"Gee whiz, Pip," he said as he doubled over into another laughing fit. "It looks as if you're not able to sleep too well. Are you just a little worried that something might happen to you if you fall asleep?"

"No!" I sort of lied. "You just woke me up when you flushed the toilet. I'm not worried about what you—"

"Well," he cut in, "half the fun is just making you worry about when I'm going to make my move!" Then he laughed so hard, he snorted like an ol' pig.

When the whistle blew the next morning, I sure wasn't ready to get up.

Yep, our camp counselor hadn't forgotten about all of those push-ups and running I was supposed to do after breakfast. Before he even counted to twenty, my back was caving in, and I couldn't even come up in one piece. I guess I looked sort of like a snake that was all bendy in the middle.

Yeah, and I could hear Joker Joey laughing his head off clear across the field. By the time I finished my tenth lap, I was ready to choke that rotten laughing hyena. I knew if it was the last thing I ever did, I was going to make sure that stinking joker got caught in one of his own tricks.

That whole morning I kept my eye on Joker Joey. I was never quite sure what that darn kid would do next. So I was surprised when we played volleyball and nothing happened.

Then Counselor Conrad told us that we'd get to go canoeing on the lake after we had lunch, but first we had to go back to our cabins and clean up.

"Hey, Pip!" shouted Joker Joey as he tore through a big, black bag he'd stashed in his suitcase. "Wait till you see what I'm planning for my next prank."

"I don't wanna know," I grumbled.

"Hope you don't feel left out, kid," he said, laughing, "cuz I haven't forgotten about you. You'll get yours when you least expect it!"

Then he grabbed a small hand drill from his bag and held it up like it was a great big prize. "There it is!" he shouted. "My next big prank is about to take place!"

I tried to eat my lunch, but I kept looking out the window. I was just wondering what that rotten kid was up to.

When I saw him sneak over to the canoes, I tried to get Counselor Conrad to look out the window too. I sure hoped that maybe he'd see that ol' joker sneaking around the canoes with his drill.

"Hey," I said, while I was looking out the window, "I wonder why Joey is getting so close to the canoes."

I was glad when our camp counselor finally

came over to the window. "Hmmm," he said. "It looks to me like Joey is just real eager to go canoeing."

Then Counselor Conrad blew his darn whistle, so we all lined up. Even Joker Joey came running. I saw him tuck his drill into the top of his pants, and he winked at me as he pulled his shirt over the top of it.

Our canoes were all numbered with the same numbers as our rooms. So that meant we had to be partners with our bunk buddies.

Yeah, it sure didn't make me too happy to know I'd have to share my canoe with that stinking joker. But I was pretty sure that he wouldn't do anything to his own canoe, so I thought maybe it was okay being with Joker Joey after all.

Our camp counselor handed us our life jackets and showed us how to put them on. He told us to keep them on at all times.

"Yep," whispered that joker, "you never know what might spring up. Ha! Ha!"

We were about halfway out on the lake when I noticed that my shoes were getting soaked.

"What the—?" I started to say, but I got cut off by that dirty rotten joker's snorting laugh.

"Ha!" roared Joey. "I bet you never thought I'd drill a hole in our boat too."

Joker Joey rocked back and forth holding onto his sides while he practically laughed his face off.

"It's like this, Pip, ol' buddy. If you don't include yourself, everyone will know who did it. Yeah, I'll bet you weren't expecting this. You better get ready to swim!" he shouted as he jumped in the water.

Just before I jumped out of the canoe, I heard the other kids shouting, and I watched them all splash into the water.

The water was ice cold, but I was steaming mad.

Nobody looked too happy when they got out of the lake all dripping wet.

Yep, Counselor Conrad looked madder than anyone. He was making a growling sound as he sloshed his way over to me.

"This better not be another one of your pranks, Pip!" he hollered at me through his teeth.

I looked over at ol' Joker Joey and noticed something he hadn't even thought about. His wet T-shirt was stuck to the drill he'd hidden underneath it. Yeah, you could see the whole outline of the crank and handle right through his soaked shirt.

"No, sir," I said, "but you can see for yourself who has the drill that made the holes in our canoes." Then I pointed over to Joker Joey.

"What's that under your shirt, Joey?" Counselor Conrad asked.

Joker Joey's mouth just hung open like a big ol' bass that just got hooked.

Well, that darn joker finally got caught, and boy, his parents didn't look too happy about having to come back and get him so early.

Yep, Joker Joey wasn't laughing at all when his father grabbed him by the arm and put him in the backseat of their car. He didn't look like he'd ever want to trick anyone again—at least not for a long time.

Our camp counselor told me that there better not be any more problems with my next bunk buddy.

I hoped real hard that there wouldn't be any more problems either. I sure needed to get some sleep.

I guess I shouldn't have put sugar on Joker Joey's fries, but I was only trying to pay him back for putting salt in the sugar bowl.

Yeah, but it sure did make me smile when Joker Joey got caught with the drill showing right through his wet shirt.

It just isn't easy being a kid. Yep, and going to camp with a bunch of stinking kids really isn't much fun.

4

A Scavenger Hunt with Cheater Chaz

The only time I got any sleep was when my bunk buddies were sent home. So when that darn whistle blew, I started hoping real hard that maybe Counselor Conrad would forget about me needing another bunk buddy. But that's when I got my worst surprise.

After we'd all lined up, our camp counselor walked up to me and shook his head real funny-like. "Well, Pip," he said, "let's see if we can give you a bunk buddy who might actually want to stay with you the rest of your time here."

Then he put his face right up next to mine and said, "They say the third time is the charm. But in your case, three strikes and you're out!"

If "out" meant I got to go home, then I was glad. Yeah, I wished real hard that I could go home early. But I guess I shouldn't have smiled again.

"Hmmm . . ." Counselor Conrad scratched his big ol' chin. "It seems to me that you might be too happy about being sent home. So let me rephrase that. I'll just make you wish you could go home even more, after I get done putting you through cleanup duty."

I gulped real hard. I sure didn't want to do cleanup duty. I was going to do my best to like my next bunk buddy.

Our camp counselor cleared his throat and then said the one thing I never wanted to hear.

"Since poor Chaz here," he said, pointing to that cheater, "had his bunk buddy go home with the flu, I'm going to move him in with you."

"What?" I nearly choked to death. But when our camp counselor looked at me, I just looked down at a gopher hole next to my foot and wished real hard that I could fit inside of it.

When I finally looked up, ol' Chaz wasn't looking too happy either. Oh yeah, I knew I was really in for it.

When we got back to our room, Chaz just grumbled like a big, mean bear. "If you can mind your own business and try not to get me into trouble again, maybe we can stick it out until it's time to leave this rotten place."

That sounded good to me, so I agreed to get along with that ol' cheater. I was even thinking it might not be so bad and maybe that stinking kid had even learned a lesson when he'd gotten caught cheating on his test last spring.

The whistle blew, so we lined up for the next activity. We were all supposed to go on some goofy-sounding hunt I'd never heard of before. It was called a *scavenger hunt.*

Our camp counselor handed each team a list of nature things we had to find. The first team to find all the stuff on their list would win the prize.

Chaz got a real strange smile and whispered real mean in my ear, "Just remember what I said about minding your own business, if you know what's good for you!"

I really didn't know what he was talking about until we went back to our room for some bug spray.

Then Chaz unzipped his suitcase and pulled out a big sealed bag filled with all kinds of nature stuff. Yeah, the stuff he pulled out all looked like the same things on our scavenger hunt list.

"How'd you know what was going to be on our list?" I wanted to know.

His eyes got real thin, sort of like he was wondering if he should tell me. Then his face changed, and he looked real proud of himself. "My brother was here last year, and he saved all the stuff he'd collected so I could use it this year. Isn't that great?" He smacked me on the back. "There are only a few things we still have to find because they have to be fresh."

I didn't answer. I just stared at the things he'd spread onto the bed.

"Boy, was I ever hoping the list would be the same as my brother's list. The only problem is . . ." he said, staring at me again, "I didn't know I was going to get unlucky and wind up with you as my bunk buddy. You better not give me away again like you did in front of Mrs. Ray. I was mad when you threw that wadded up test at me and then she saw the spelling words written on my hand. I got detention for a whole week. You just better not be a tattletale this time."

I thought about that ol' tattletale I knew named Tess and shook my head. "No. I'm not a stinking tattletale."

"Well, you better not be, cuz I want us to get that prize."

"What's the prize?" I asked.

"I don't know, but last year my brother and his partner won some cool iPods."

I thought about finally having my own iPod, just like my sister, K.D., had. That would be really cool. *Yeah*, I thought, *maybe this time letting him cheat might be sort of okay.* "All right, I'm in," I said.

"Good!" He gave me a fist bump, and then

he smiled real big. "I guess we're partners this time. But we better get going since we still have to find a live beetle, five berries, and an insect-eaten leaf."

Yeah, his scary smile sort of creeped me out. But that prize sounded pretty nice. I guess Chaz was still a great big cheater. Yep, I sure didn't feel too good about being partners with Cheater Chaz.

After we'd put all of our stuff into the sack Counselor Conrad gave us, we ran into the woods to find the things we still needed.

I knew it wouldn't be too hard to find the beetle because they were all over the place. Yep, there was a big fat one crawling over an old log right next to my leg. I picked it up and stuck it in a plastic jar with holes in it, so it wouldn't kill him, or anything. Then I put the jar in our sack and took off to see what Cheater Chaz was hollering about.

"Hey, Pip," he shouted, "come see these berries." He pointed to some pink and orange berries on the side of the road. "Do you think those are the right kind of berries?"

"Hmmm. They look just like the picture our camp counselor showed us, so let's pick five of them and put them in that plastic bag in our sack."

"Now," said that cheater, "we just need to find a leaf that's been eaten by some insect."

"Why don't we just pick some big ol' leaf, and give it to the beetle I found, so he can chew on it?" I asked.

Chaz gave me a real hard slap on the back. "Now you're thinking like a pro."

I wasn't sure that was such a good thing—especially if I was making some rotten cheater proud of me.

But that ol' beetle didn't seem real interested in eating the leaf I'd stuck in his jar. We watched him walk over the leaf and under the leaf. He didn't even take one bite off it.

"Gee, maybe he's just not hungry," I said.

"Who cares?" Cheater Chaz grumbled. Then he got a real crazy look on his face. "How would Counselor Conrad know if it was an insect that ate the leaf or a kid taking tiny bites?"

So he grabbed a clump of three leaves and held them up for me to see. "These three green leaves look good enough to eat, don't they?"

"Well, maybe," I said, "but isn't there some rule about 'Leaves of three, let them be'? So we should probably leave those alone."

"Ah, Pip, you're such a scaredy-cat. They don't even have any red on them, do they? So they can't be poisonous." He pulled one of the three leaves off. "I'm just gonna take a few tiny bites so it looks like a bug chewed on it."

Before I could say anything else, that darn kid took a couple of bug-sized bites off that leaf.

"Yuck!" He spit out leaf pieces everywhere. "That was just nasty!"

Then he stuck that bitten leaf into another little bag and put it into our sack.

"Well," he said, laughing, "it looks like we are the winners. Just look at all of those goofy kids running around trying to find everything we've already found."

"We didn't really find everything ourselves . . ." I started to say.

"Oh, who cares? We're gonna get the prize, and that's all that counts." Then he looked real nervous. "And you better not tell anyone about this, or I'll tell everyone at school that you're just a great big tattletale."

Nope, I sure didn't want kids to call me a tattletale. So I told him that I wouldn't tell anyone.

The ol' cheater said we'd probably look suspicious if we turned in our scavenger stuff too soon. So we waited for about fifteen minutes before we went to find our camp counselor.

Oh yeah, Counselor Conrad was real surprised when we brought him our sack and showed him our checked-off list. He blew his darn whistle and blasted out my ear again. Then he hollered for everyone to come back and stop their scavenger hunting.

"It looks like we have a winner," he said when everyone was standing around us. "And this just might be a new record!"

All of the kids made moaning noises. I sure felt guilty.

"Well," he said, shaking his head, "nothing is definite until I've seen what they have in their sack."

He took our sack over to a picnic table and

pulled out all the little plastic bags, plus our bug jar. "Hmmm. It looks like it's all here." Then he named each thing on our list and held the items up, saying what each thing was and shouting "check" each time.

When he got to our last bag, he said, "Insect eaten leaf. Ch—" But then he stopped and looked like some sort of statue.

He held up our bagged leaf and asked us if there'd been two other leaves with that one.

Cheater Chaz looked kind of nervous when he answered, "Uh, yeah, I guess."

"Which one of you found the leaf?" Counselor Conrad wanted to know.

I didn't say anything.

Finally that ol' cheater said he'd found it.

"Well, young man, you just picked yourself a poison ivy leaf."

I heard all of the other kids say, "Ohhh," at the same time.

"But the leaves didn't have red on them, so how could they be poisonous?" asked Cheater Chaz.

"The leaves are usually bright green this time of year, but they're still poisonous. Anyway, you handled poison ivy, so you better come with me to the nurse's office."

Cheater Chaz leaned over and said, "I don't feel so good. Maybe I shouldn't have eaten . . ." He stopped and looked up real worried, like maybe he said something he shouldn't have.

Our camp counselor's eyes got real squinty. "Young man, you didn't take those small bites off the leaf did you?"

I couldn't believe it. Ol' Cheater Chaz started bawling just like a big baby. Yep, he was even crying louder than that stinking Whiner Winston.

"Am I gonna die?" he wanted to know.

He was taken to the camp nurse's office and given some kind of an allergy shot that made him scream real loud.

Counselor Conrad wanted to know if I had anything to do with Chaz eating the leaf. I just told him that I'd tried to warn Chaz about the rule, "Leaves of three, let them be," but Chaz just wouldn't listen to me.

I couldn't believe it when our camp counselor patted me on my back and said, "Well, at least you remembered that rule, young man. Too bad your bunk buddy didn't listen to you."

For once Counselor Conrad was being nice to me, and I sure didn't deserve it. Boy, did I feel guilty.

No, Chaz didn't die, or anything. But he sure did get real sick, and he had blisters on his hands and mouth. His parents even had to come pick the rotten cheater up and take him home.

We didn't get the prize because our camp counselor found out that Chaz had cheated big time. That ol' cheater must have really felt like he was dying, or something, because before he went home, he confessed to everything. Yep, he even told Counselor Conrad he'd used his brother's scavenger hunt stuff. Oh yeah, and he told Counselor Conrad that I was his "partner in crime," so I got in trouble too.

I don't think I would have wanted that ol' prize anyway, since I didn't really earn it.

I heard Cheater Chaz sure was itching a whole lot. It was kind of a good lesson for an ol' cheater like Chaz. But I guess I shouldn't have listened to someone who was such a big cheater because that kind of made me a cheater too.

You know, it just isn't easy being a kid. And I was real tired of being at that darn summer camp with all of those rotten kids.

5

Target Practice
with Show-Off Shad

Well, after Cheater Chaz went home, our camp counselor called me into his office. Yeah, I was real scared. I was hoping he'd send me home too, but he had a different plan.

"Pip, I don't know what to do with you," he said. "I know I told you that after three strikes you'd be out." He scratched his head. "But you seem to want to go home, and I happen to think there's still some hope for you." He rubbed his chin a whole lot, sort of like he was thinking real hard. "Maybe you just don't do well when there's another kid who is even more mischievous than you. It's hard to say who is actually getting the other one into trouble where you're concerned . . ."

I started to say something but decided to clear my throat instead. I still wasn't sure where he was going with what he was saying. At least I had learned one thing—sometimes it's just better to zip the ol' lip.

"Anyway, Pip," he said, shaking his head, "it's now too late to add any more kids to our camp, so until we can make further accommodations, you'll just have to bunk alone."

I wasn't sure what *accommodations* were, but I didn't care. At least I didn't have to have another bunk buddy. But I guess I shouldn't have shouted "Yes!" and made a great big fist pump.

"Don't get too excited, young man," he

said. "You still owe me some cleanup duty for cheating on the scavenger hunt."

I guess I should have known our camp counselor wouldn't forget anything.

Yep, the next morning I had to pick up trash a whole hour before I even ate breakfast. I never knew there were so many stinking litter bugs. And it sure didn't help much when the wind was blowing all the stuff around, so I had to run after it before I could get it into my sack.

Yeah, I was never so glad to hear that whistle blow to line up for breakfast. I handed Counselor Conrad my sack and got into line.

"Pip!" he shouted. "I don't want your trash. Take it to the dumpster and go wash your hands. You can join us for breakfast as soon as you're done."

When I got to the mess hall, the first thing I saw was that big show-off named Shad balancing his plate of food right on top of his head. He sure didn't look too smart. I just wondered why our camp counselor never saw him when he was goofing around.

We had to go to another craft class after breakfast. I was just hoping we didn't have to glue anymore ol' pinecones onto a wreath like last time. But when I saw the girls' counselor, Counselor Becky, pass out brown construction paper and scissors, I thought we might have to do something even more boring than gluing pinecones. It turned out we were making log cabins.

When I looked over at Shad, he was pretending to cut his hair with his scissors. That's when I noticed I didn't even get any scissors. I raised my hand to let Counselor Becky know, but she was busy helping someone design a log cabin, so I went up to the desk and grabbed a pair.

I didn't want her to see me, so I ran back to my seat. But I guess I'd forgotten that all grown-ups have eyes in the back of their heads.

"Pip!" she shouted. "Don't run with sharp objects in your hands!"

I saw that show-off nod his head and mouth the words, "Nice one, Pip."

After we'd designed and cut out our log cabins, it was time to line up for relay races. That's when I found out that Bossy Billy was in detention for something bad he'd done, so I was supposed to be Show-Off Shad's partner.

When I found Shad, he was standing on his head trying to catch a bee in his mouth.

"You better stop messing around," I said. "You're supposed to run with the stick first, so let's get going."

He just yawned and told me not to be such a worrywart. Then he grabbed the stick I held out to him, and he tossed it up into the air. He did some kind of crazy twirling turn, caught the stick with his other hand, and took a bow before he took off running.

When it was my turn to run, he threw the stick at me. Luckily I caught it. I had to run extra fast to make up for all the time he'd wasted showing off. I ran so fast that I didn't see the gopher hole on the other side of the finish line. Yep, down I went when my toe got stuck.

Boy, did that get everyone laughing. My face sure did feel hot.

Shad came over and gave me a high five. "Gee, Pip, I've tried everything I could think of to make those kids laugh. I didn't know that all I really had to do was just trip. I guess I forgot that the funniest stunt of all is just watching people fall down. Ha! Thanks for giving me a great idea!"

I was going to ask him why he always had

to do something goofy just to try to make everyone laugh, but he was already walking away on his hands.

After lunch we were supposed to learn how to shoot arrows at targets. It was some sport called *archery.* I was kind of glad we were going to finally do something that sounded fun and not something silly like making things out of pinecones, cutting out log cabins, or running with sticks.

I looked over at Shad, who'd taken an apple from our lunch table and was balancing it on top of his head.

"Hey, who wants to play William Tell and shoot an arrow through the apple?" he asked.

Nobody looked too interested except Counselor Conrad, who was looking at me sort of like he expected me to do something that stupid.

"Just remember, boys and girls," he said,

"we only aim at the targets we have set up. Anybody who shoots at anything else will find themselves in a heap of trouble!"

I really didn't know why he had to keep looking at me while he told us that. He must really think I'm dumb. The only one who'd probably shoot an arrow into an apple sitting on someone's head was Show-Off Shad. And even I couldn't figure out how he'd be able to shoot an arrow into an apple that was sitting on his own head.

But that ol' show-off was kind of smart when it came to figuring out how to do crazy things.

I saw him take his turn shooting the bow and arrow with our camp counselor. Yeah, I was really surprised to see his arrows even make it onto the board. Then I watched him grab an arrow out of the bag and stick it up his sleeve while Counselor Conrad added up his score.

Oh yeah, he was a real sneak. I guess I could call him Sneaky Shad. But he's more of a show-off than anything else, so I decided to just keep calling him Show-Off Shad.

Anyway, it sure did bug me because nobody ever seemed to see the rotten kids do anything bad. Nope! But if I did anything even halfway bad, I always got caught.

Well, I took my turn and even got a *bull's-eye*. Our camp counselor said that's when the arrow hits the very middle of the target.

Counselor Conrad raised his eyebrows and told me, "Good eye, Pip!"

Boy, was I happy. Yeah, I couldn't believe it; I was finally having some fun, and Counselor Conrad was even being nice to me.

But things weren't so great when we went to dinner. That darn Show-Off Shad came into the mess hall moaning, hardly able to walk.

Then after we all turned around to look at

him, I saw the worst thing I've ever seen. The poor kid had an arrow sticking in his side. You should have heard all of the screams from everyone sitting around the tables. I don't even know for sure, but I might have screamed too.

Counselor Conrad came running from the front of the mess hall. "Don't move, Shad!" he shouted. "And I don't want anyone to touch him. He could bleed to death if you pull the arrow out!"

Our mouths just hung open as Shad pulled that arrow out from under his arm and said, "You mean like this?"

Gee, he was almost as rotten as Joker Joey. But Show-Off Shad wasn't mean. He was just a big ol', stinking show-off.

"See?" he said as he held it up in the air. "I'm not really hurt. I was just having fun with all of you.

Our camp counselor sure wasn't in the

mood to laugh. I'll bet when Show-Off Shad saw the look in Counselor Conrad's eyes, he was wishing he really did have an arrow in his side.

Then the very worst thing really did happen. That darn show-off pretended to trip with the arrow still in his hand. We couldn't believe it, but he really did fall right onto his own arrow. Boy, did Counselor Conrad look sick when he saw the arrow was really sticking out of that kid's side. He hollered at Counselor Becky to call 911. Then he told everyone to just stay in their seats—everyone except me. He told me to run and get the camp nurse. I couldn't believe he asked me to help out.

It seemed like forever before the paramedics arrived, but at least our camp nurse brought blankets. "To keep him from going into shock," she told us.

The good news was that the arrow hadn't

gone in too deep, and the counselors told us he'd soon be as good as he was before. I was kind of hoping he'd be better than he was before.

I guess I might have given Show-Off Shad the idea to trip and fall to get a laugh. But I sure didn't fall on purpose like he did.

Yeah, I'm glad Shad wasn't hurt worse. But he sure shouldn't have played with that darn arrow.

I probably should have told the camp counselor that Show-Off Shad had taken one of the arrows. Counselor Conrad would have taken it away from him, and then he wouldn't have gotten hurt.

Well, at least that big ol' show-off let us all see how dangerous it is to play with sharp things. Kind of like when Counselor Becky told me not to run with sharp objects. I'm never going to do that again.

Yep, it sure isn't easy being a kid, especially when there are so many things that can hurt us, even when we're just trying to have some fun.

6

Tug-of-War with Bossy Billy

The next morning, I was kind of scared. I just knew that our camp counselor would tell me that I'd have to bunk with that rotten Bossy Billy because his bunk buddy had bailed.

Yep, my stomach sure did get into one big ol' knot when Counselor Conrad called me over after breakfast.

"Pip!" he said in kind of a tough way. "Why is it that wherever you go, trouble always seems to follow?"

I didn't know if he really wanted me to answer that question, and it looked like he had more to say, so I just kept my mouth shut.

"It just amazes me that every kid you've ever partnered up with has been sent home." He looked at me with those squinty eyes that always mean I'm in for it, and then he asked me another question I didn't know if I was supposed to answer. "Can you give me any reason for this?"

"Well . . ." I tried hard to think of the right answer. "Maybe there are just a whole lot of bad kids at this camp," I said.

I don't know if he liked my answer, but his mouth did look like he wanted to smile.

"Yeah, maybe you're right. But I'm not taking any chances next time," he said. "Hmmm, I have to put you with somebody. You know we can't have two people who are without bunk buddies. It's just not economical."

"Eco—what?" I asked.

He looked at me kind of funny and shook his head. "Pip, it just means we can't spend the extra money on separate rooms when we could put two kids in the same bunk room." He rubbed his chin, like he always did when he looked like he was thinking real hard. "And something tells me you and Billy wouldn't work out too well as bunk buddies. So that gives us a bit of a problem."

"Gee," I said, "maybe you should just send us both home."

"You really want out of here, don't you?"

"Well, only if it will help you out." I tried to smile.

He pulled on some little hairs that were starting to grow on his chin. "Listen here, Pip, I happen to think this camp will help you to become a more *mature* young man."

Yeah, there was that stinking *mature* word

again. I wondered why grown-ups can't just let me be a kid.

"I'll need to think on this awhile," he said. Then he grabbed my shoulder, sort of like my dad does, and said we'd talk about it after lunch.

When we finished our morning exercises, we were told that both the boys and the girls had to practice for something called a *talent show*.

Yep, we were supposed to all do something like sing, dance, or play an instrument. I'm not good at any of those things. But we were supposed to have a show ready by Saturday because our parents were all going to be there for it.

I heard that bossy kid telling the shy girl named Shannon that if she wanted to be his talent show partner, then she'd better listen to what he said. I kind of felt sorry for her.

"Hey, Shannon," I said, "I don't have a partner, so do you wanna be my talent show partner?"

She sure didn't look too happy. I don't think she thought I'd be much nicer than Bossy Billy.

"Bud out, kid!" Bossy Billy said to me.

"What's the matter with you?" I asked. "We get to pick who we want for our partners. So if Shannon wants me to be her partner, then it's up to her."

Shy Shannon didn't look like she knew what she wanted. I could hardly even hear her when she whispered, "Aren't you the kid who put salt in my cocoa?"

"Nope!" I said. "That wasn't me. It was that darn joker named Joey who did that."

She lifted her shoulders and quietly said, "Okay."

"Aw, who cares?" said Bossy Billy. "You

probably don't have any talent anyway. You're both just losers!"

Boy, was I angry. But I saw our camp counselor watching us, so I decided not to even answer that darn kid.

"So what do you want to do in the talent show?" I asked that shy girl.

She lifted her shoulders up again and said, "I don't know."

Yeah, I was real mad at myself for feeling sorry for her. I knew I got stuck with someone who probably wasn't talented at all. Sort of like me.

"Well," I said, trying to get her to talk, "just pretend you had something you could do, what would it be?"

Shy Shannon just looked at the ground and whispered, "I guess I would sing, if I could."

"That's great!" I tried to sound real happy. "I wish I could play the guitar. So maybe you can pretend you're singing and I can pretend to be playing the guitar."

Counselor Conrad heard me talking to that shy girl and told me he had a good idea. He said he'd brought his guitar and I could use it if I wanted to.

When I told him I didn't really know how to play, he said he'd show me where to put my fingers on something called *frets,* and then I could just pretend to strum along. I tried, but I wasn't too good.

"Don't 'fret' about it, Pip," he told me, laughing at his own joke.

Shy Shannon looked more scared than I was feeling. She tried to sing, but no words came out.

That's when Counselor Becky came over. She said Shannon could pretend to sing along to a CD she'd brought. She told us when you moved your mouth to a song and no words came out, it was something called *lip-syncing*. I was just hoping I could do some *guitar-syncing*.

We both had to practice pretending to sing and play the guitar to some song Counselor Becky brought us, called, "You've Got a Friend," by somebody I never heard of named Carole King.

Boy, was I glad when it was time for lunch.

After lunch Counselor Conrad told me that he knew he was right in thinking I wouldn't get along with Billy. So he said he'd switch it so I bunked with someone named Nam.

Then our camp counselor took me over to that kid named Nam. He told him who I was, and he asked us to shake hands. I was kind of nervous because the last time I shook someone's hand, I got buzzed by that darn Joker Joey.

But nothing happened, so I was real glad.

Yeah, I was really hoping that maybe he'd be okay.

A little later Counselor Conrad told us that we were going to play a game called *tug-of-war*. We had to play with the girls, not against them. He said he'd mix the teams to keep them fair.

When I saw the counselors digging a hole and filling it with water to make mud, I was pretty sure we were going to have a good time.

Then they took out a real long, thick rope and laid it across that hole. They told us that we were supposed to pull the other team into that muddy hole.

"After you're done, you can shower off in the outside showers," said our camp counselor.

Everyone looked real worried.

"Of course, you will keep your clothes on when you use the outside showers," he added.

Yeah, that sure made all of us laugh.

Then they called out "girl, boy, girl," and kept going until all of us had a team.

That stinking Bossy Billy was on my team. He told everyone that he wanted to be the kid at the front because he was stronger than any of us. Yep, he sure thought he was something really great.

Shy Shannon was put behind Bossy Billy, and I had to be behind Shy Shannon. She didn't look too happy to be right in the middle of us. But we had to stay where we were, so we just grabbed the rope and starting pulling when the whistle blew.

"Come on!" shouted Bossy Billy. "Pull harder!"

Shannon's face was real red and puffy. I could tell she was pulling her hardest.

That darn bossy kid shouted even louder, "What's the matter? Are you all a bunch of wimps?"

"Hey, Billy!" I yelled back. "Why don't you shut up?"

Of course, Counselor Conrad was coming up right next to me, and he must've heard me say "shut up."

"Pip! There's no need for that kind of talk around here. Work as a team. I better not hear anymore fighting," he said.

Nope! He didn't even hear that rotten ol' bossy kid call us wimps. He just heard me when I got mad and said "shut up." I knew it was time for a payback. That Bossy Billy needed a lesson.

Yeah, I had another great idea. If he wanted to call us all mean names, then we needed to show him what we could do.

So I turned around and told the kid behind me to "stop pulling," and to pass it on to the rest of our team. Then I whispered to Shannon to let go too.

Yep, our team all let go of the rope, except for Bossy Billy. We just stood there with our mouths hanging open as that rotten kid went flying right into the mud hole.

Boy, was that the funniest thing I'd ever seen! Bossy Billy's face was dripping with mud. It was even coming out of his mouth.

Oh yeah, both teams laughed real hard.

"What's going on here?" our camp counselor wanted to know.

That ol' bossy kid pointed to our team, spit out a whole lot of mud, and then said, "They let go of the rope."

"Now why in the world would your team let go of the rope?" Counselor Conrad looked at me. "A team is called a 'team' because they're supposed to work together."

Then he walked right up to me and asked, "What happened?"

"He called us all wimps," I said.

"Why would you do that, Billy?" he asked.

"Because they're all a bunch of good-for-nothing losers!" Billy shouted through his muddy teeth.

I couldn't believe it when that rotten kid scooped up a big ol' clump of mud and threw it at all of us. Shy Shannon was the closest to him, so she got most of it in her hair.

That made me really mad. "You leave Shannon alone!" I yelled.

"Oooh, Pip's got a crush on Shannon." He laughed real hard. "Two losers go together!"

My face got real hot. I rushed over to that mud hole and pushed Bossy Billy's head right down into the mud. "Don't call us losers!"

Counselor Conrad and Counselor Becky jumped into the mud and pulled us apart before a real big fight started.

Yeah, I sure did get in trouble. But so did Bossy Billy. Our camp counselor told us that we both "behaved badly," and we weren't supposed to get into fights. He said we should learn to use words that can fix things and not use *put-down words* like "wimp" and "loser."

Nobody was sent home. We were told to go wash off in the outside showers and then do ten laps each.

When we got near the outside of one of the showers, we heard singing. It was a real nice sound, sort of like birds, only better. It was that song "You've Got a Friend"—the same song Shy Shannon and I had been practicing.

That's when the weirdest of all things happened. The water stopped, and I almost fainted when I saw it was Shy Shannon who got out.

She looked surprised to see us too. Yep, she turned bright red and ran all the way back to the girls' cabins.

Ol' Bossy Billy and I just stared at each other, like we couldn't believe what we'd just seen.

"Who knew she could sing?" he asked.

"Wow!" was all I could say back.

We didn't say one word as we showered the mud off or while we ran our ten laps. I guess we were just too shocked to even talk.

Yeah, Counselor Conrad lectured us pretty good, and he kept using that darn *mature* word. But I didn't care. I just thought about how Shy Shannon could really sing, and I didn't feel so bad anymore.

I guess I shouldn't have said "shut up." And I probably shouldn't have shoved ol' Bossy Billy's head in the mud, even if he did deserve it.

Hey, it's just not that easy being a kid. And I sure was glad that I only had a few more days of summer camp left. Yeah, that made me feel a whole lot better.

7

Haiku with Corrector Cora

It sure was good to have Nam for my bunk buddy. Yeah, Nam was a pretty smart kid, maybe even kind of a nerd. I could've called him Nerdy Nam, but that didn't sound very nice, so I decided to call him Normal Nam. He was really normal in a good sort of way.

Yep, we stayed up half the night talking and laughing, so I was real tired when that darn whistle blew that morning.

Our camp counselor looked real worried when he saw my sleepy face.

He asked me, "So how are you and Nam doing together?"

He looked real glad when I said, "Oh, he's great!"

Gee, I guess he didn't think I would ever get along with anyone at that darn camp.

We all had to practice some more for our talent show.

Shy Shannon still wouldn't sing in front of me. I guess she only liked to sing in the shower.

"Shannon," I said, "I know you can sing. So what's the big deal?"

"I don't know," she said so quietly I could hardly hear her. "Maybe I can only sing in the shower."

"Well, you've got to try." I shook my head. "Look at me. I can't play the guitar, but at least I'm trying."

"I don't really have to sing, and you don't

really have to play the guitar," she whispered, "because we can play the CD." Then she put her head down like she always did.

"Well," I told her, "you've got to at least move your mouth to the words. And you better lift your head up so people can see your face."

She shook her head. "I just don't know if I can sing in front of an audience."

"Why don't you just pretend nobody is there? Or just think of them all doing something really weird."

I sure did feel sorry for Shy Shannon. Yeah, especially when I saw big ol' tears in her pretty green eyes. Oops! Did I say pretty? I sure didn't mean to say anything that crazy. But it sure did bug me that she was so darn scared of everything.

After we got done with practice, we had to play tennis. I'd never played before, so I wasn't very good. I was kind of hoping I'd get

Nam for my partner, but they gave me this girl named Cora.

"Well, Pip," she said in a real snooty voice, "I can see you've never done this before. You're holding your racket all wrong."

Then she pulled the racket from my hand and squeezed my fingers to put them back where she wanted them. Boy, did I feel dumb.

"Don't you even know what a backhand is!" she screamed at me.

I just couldn't wait for that tennis game to end so I wouldn't have to listen to her mean voice telling me what I was doing wrong all the time.

When I hit the stinking ball into the net, she acted like it was the worst thing she'd ever seen.

"What's the matter with you?" she yelled. "Can't you do anything right?"

Boy, was I mad. I just pretended not to hear

her. Yeah, her big ol' mouth kept moving, but I sure wasn't listening.

When we lost, I didn't even care. I was just so glad that I didn't have to see that loud mouth flapping anymore.

But after lunch, I found out we had to do something even worse than play tennis.

Our camp counselor said we were going to learn poetry. I sure wasn't too happy because I thought poetry was one of the worst things ever invented.

Then we had to listen to Counselor Becky talk for one whole hour about the different kinds of poetry. Yeah, I thought there were just two kinds of poetry: dumb and dumber.

I was even more upset when we had to go into groups and they told us we had to write a *haiku* about some kind of *camp experience.*

My group started out pretty good because I was with Normal Nam and Shy Shannon.

Then Counselor Becky asked us if we could also let Cora into our group because she didn't have anyone to work with her. I wanted to scream!

I sure could have told Counselor Becky why she didn't have anyone to work with— because who wanted to work with a big-mouth corrector?

Right away Corrector Cora had to act like she was some kind of teacher, and she asked, "So, Pip, why don't you give us an example of haiku?"

I felt my face get real hot, and I said something like, "There was an old woman who lived in a shoe; she had so many children she didn't know what to do . . ."

"No, no, no!" shouted Corrector Cora. "That's not haiku!"

"I was just kidding," I said. "Geez, do you have to always be so darn serious?"

Normal Nam put his hands over his mouth. He looked like he was trying to hold in a big ol' laugh.

When I looked at Shy Shannon, she sort of smiled, and then she put her head down.

"Well," growled that darn corrector, "if you were listening to Counselor Becky, you'd know all about haiku." Then she made a real ugly sound. I guess she was trying to clear her throat, or something.

"Haiku has three lines with seventeen syllables. There are five syllables in the first, seven in the second, and five in the third." Then she looked over at me and asked, "You do know what syllables are, don't you?"

"Yeah, I know what they are," I said. "They use them in the band. You know, they're the two big, shiny, round things they bang together."

Boy, did that make my two friends laugh.

That was the first time I'd heard Shy Shannon laugh. It was kind of a silly giggle, but it sounded really great.

"Oh, come on!" shouted Corrector Cora. "You can't be that dumb!"

"I can too!" I hollered without thinking.

At least my friends thought I was just kidding, so they laughed some more. Nam made a big roaring sound, sort of like a big ol' lion. Shannon's head was down, but I saw her shoulders moving up and down, so I knew she was laughing too.

"Well, just in case you've got one ounce of a brain, I'm going to try to help you learn haiku."

I sure didn't like the way she said that, but I thought I better listen anyway.

So she gave us a bunch of examples, then said, "And for those who still don't know what a syllable is"—she looked right at me—"it's how we divide up a word. For example, my name is Cora, and it has two syllables: Cor-uh."

She was kind of tall for a girl, so she bent over and asked me very slowly, "So, Pip, how many syllables are in your name?"

"One," I mumbled.

"Very good, Pip!" she said in her best teacher's voice.

"Hey, stop talking to me like I'm some kind of dummy."

"Well, when you can stop acting like a dummy, then I'll stop talking to you like you're a dummy. Now, where was I?"

Her big ol' mouth kept moving some more, and I started not to hear her words again.

Then she made us all practice. That stinking corrector sure thought she was smart. But I think I'd rather not be such a stinking smarty-pants because nobody seemed to like her very much.

After Shy Shannon tried her haiku, Corrector Cora said in a real mean voice, "Speak up. Nobody can ever hear you!"

"Hey!" I shouted. "Just leave us alone! We can all work a lot better without you bugging us about every darn thing we say and do!"

I looked up to see Counselor Conrad looking back at me. "Pi-i-ip!" he shouted across the room.

"I guess I was wrong, Cora." I laughed. "It sounds like my name has three syllables when my camp counselor says it."

She didn't look like she thought I was very funny, but I sure didn't care.

Counselor Becky told us that our group time was over, and we all had to return to our seats and write our haikus.

I was sure glad to get away from that stinking corrector, but I was kind of scared about having to make up my own haiku. I didn't know what to write about. I just thought poetry was so dumb.

That sort of gave me an idea. So after our counselors passed out a piece of paper to each of us, I wrote:

"Poetry's dumb."

I didn't even know it, but ol' Corrector Cora was sitting right behind me. She tapped me on my shoulder and said, "That's only four syllables." And then she sounded it out. "Po-e-try's dumb. You better fix that!"

"Then I'll just add 'so' to it," I said. "Poetry's so dumb."

"No talking!" shouted Counselor Conrad, looking right at me.

"Can I move somewhere else?" I asked.

"You can go sit over there." He pointed to a sunny spot by the window. "But you better get to work. We only have twelve minutes left.

Well, that rotten corrector had given me an

even better idea for my haiku. Yep, I erased the stuff I'd written and wrote a new haiku. I didn't stop until I was done. The alarm went off a few minutes later, so the other kids stopped too.

Then I got my next surprise. Counselor Becky told us we had to read our haiku in front of the class. I couldn't believe it. Yeah, it was too late to change anything. Oh boy, did I feel sick.

Of course Corrector Cora asked if she could read what she wrote first. So she cleared her throat and read:

"Birds singing softly,

Pine needles crunch underfoot,

Strolling through the woods."

The camp counselors clapped for her, like it was the best thing they'd ever heard.

Shy Shannon whispered her whole poem, so nobody even knew what she'd written. I guess that wasn't such a bad idea.

Next, ol' Bossy Billy read his haiku about leadership:

"Camp taught me about leading.

We all need to lead . . ."

For some crazy reason, he looked over at me before he read his last line:

"Without being too bossy."

I clapped real loud for him. I was thinking that maybe that bossy kid had really learned some kind of a lesson.

But Corrector Cora jumped out of her seat. "He said it all wrong! It's supposed to be five-seven-five and not seven-five-seven!"

I was sure right about that ol' corrector always correcting everybody. I couldn't believe she even corrected Bossy Billy.

Then I heard my name. "Pip!" Counselor Conrad called out. "Pip, stop daydreaming. It's your turn."

When I stood up to read my haiku, I felt

my legs shake really bad. But I had to do it, so I read:

"Cora just corrects.

It must make her feel so smart.

No kids like Cora."

When I was done, everyone just stared. They looked like a room full of zombies. Corrector Cora's mouth just kept opening and closing like a big ol' fish.

After what seemed like forever, our camp counselor said, "Pip, I need you to step outside for a little chat."

Oh yeah, I knew I was in big trouble. Yep, he told me how it's wrong to make others feel bad and that we weren't supposed to say mean things about the other kids in our poems.

Then he just looked at me real serious-like and asked me, "What do you have to say for yourself?"

"Gee," I said, "my poem was five-seven-five.

Aren't you proud of me for making my first haiku?"

Counselor Conrad just threw his hands up in the air and said, "I give up!"

When we got back to our room, my bunk buddy, Normal Nam, gave me a great big high five and a pat on the back. "Way to go, Pip! That was the best haiku of all. At least you finally made Cora speechless."

"Thanks," I said, but I didn't really feel so great.

Before I went to bed, I thought about my rotten day. Maybe I shouldn't have gotten so darn mad at Corrector Cora.

Yeah, I just don't think kids like being corrected all of the time—especially by another kid. But I probably shouldn't have said that no kids liked her, even if it was sort of true. I guess it was kind of mean to say that in my haiku.

Yep, it sure isn't easy being a kid. But for some strange reason I didn't mind being at summer camp so much anymore. And I really didn't know why.

8

A Spelling Bee with Normal Nam

After we ate breakfast, we were all told we had to do something I hated more than anything. Yep, our camp counselors told us that we had to have a contest called a *spelling bee*.

I couldn't believe it. We were going to have to do something even worse than poetry. Oh yeah, spelling was the very worst thing in the whole wide world.

"You will be partnering up with your bunk

buddies," said Counselor Conrad. "It's a little different version of the actual game because you will get an extra point if your partner can first give you the definition of the word you will spell. But you will still play as individuals, boys versus girls."

"What?" I shouted.

"Excuse me, Pip, I was talking. If you have a question, then please raise your hand."

My hand shot straight up, but I asked my question at the same time. "I don't get it. How do we win?"

"Well, Pip," said our camp counselor, "if you'd let me finish, I was about to get to that."

Then he looked over at Counselor Becky and asked her if she could explain the rules. "She's probably better at this than I am," he said.

So she told us the rules, and that we only could use our partners for the meaning of the words, which gave us an extra point. But each partner would play against the team on the other side, which would mean "girls against boys."

She told us partners could still help each other with the *definitions*, even when they were out of the game because they'd missed a spelling word.

"So," said Counselor Becky, "the last man standing wins!" Then she sort of laughed. "I mean the last girl or boy standing wins."

"Remember," said Counselor Conrad, "you will get extra points for the definitions, which I will record. But the winner must be able to spell every word correctly. So we will have two prizes, one for the team with the most definitions correct, and the other for the best speller. Got it?" he asked, looking right at me.

I sort of understood, but I thought I better not ask any more questions. I was just lucky to have a smart kid like Normal Nam as my partner.

When it was finally our turn, all of the girls had already beaten all of the boys before us. I sure didn't know why most girls are better at spelling than boys. I was thinking that maybe it was because they probably used a lot more words to say things than most boys did. Yeah, they sure do talk a whole lot. Yep, the only girl I'd ever known who doesn't like to talk was Shy Shannon.

Well, our word was "intelligent." I was supposed to spell it first, so Normal Nam gave me the definition. It meant to be super smart.

I thought real hard. Then I sounded it out in my head.

"Okay," I said, "i-n-t-e-l . . ." I was really trying hard, but I couldn't remember if it had two *l*'s or one.

"Why don't you just give up?" said that

stinking ol' Corrector. "The word is probably too 'intelligent' for you to say."

Counselor Becky sure was mad. She told Corrector Cora she was not allowed to use *put-downs* and that she'd be out of the game if she said one more word when it wasn't her turn.

Boy, did that zip her lip. I was real glad to see that rotten kid finally get in trouble.

"Pip," said Counselor Becky, "I'm sorry about the disturbance. You may start over again."

So I tried spelling that darn word again. I sounded it out in my head. I still couldn't hear if it had one or two *l*'s, but I just went for it. "I-n-t-e-l-i-j-e-n-t."

"Sorry, Pip, that is incorrect." Counselor Becky looked kind of sad for me. "I think you might have gotten the word correct if you hadn't been interrupted."

"Good try," said Normal Nam. Then he spelled the word. "I-n-t-e-l-l-i-g-e-n-t."

"Correct!" shouted both camp counselors.

I was happy for him, so I said, "Way to go!" Then I quietly added, "I thought I heard a 'j' sound."

"The 'g' makes a 'j' sound when it's in front of the 'e'," he whispered back.

When they gave him a new word, I couldn't believe the word was "mature." And Normal Nam had to go up against Shy Shannon.

Yeah, her partner didn't even know the definition.

Yep, poor Shannon—nobody could even hear what she was trying to spell. Our camp counselors kept giving her chances to spell it louder, but she just couldn't do it.

They finally had to tell her that she didn't get the word, and they gave it to Normal Nam.

I sure was excited when I got to give the definition. I told him, "The word means 'to grow.'"

I saw Counselor Conrad nod his head and smile at me.

Of course, good ol' Normal Nam spelled it just right. But I could tell he felt sad for Shy Shannon.

Then it was Corrector Cora's turn. Her word was some word I'd never heard before; it was "judgmental."

Her partner told her it meant, "Someone who makes quick decisions about someone else." Then she whispered real loud, "Kind of like you do."

I almost laughed out loud. Yep, I had to work real hard to swallow that big laugh of mine.

Corrector Cora sure didn't look happy. "That's easy," she said. "J-u-d-g-e-m-e-n-t-e-l."

"Sorry," said Counselor Becky, "that's incorrect."

Yeah, Normal Nam spelled it without wasting any time at all: "J-u-d-g-m-e-n-t-a-l."

He was right again. I sure was proud of my new friend, so I gave him a great big pat on the back. Then I looked over and saw Counselor Conrad smiling at me again. Yeah, he even gave me two giant thumbs-up.

Yep, it turned out to be a pretty good game after all. I sure was glad that Normal Nam ended up the last kid standing.

We didn't win the team prize for the most definitions, because I only knew one word: "mature." But I was still happy for my friend Nam, who won the spelling bee.

When we finished with lunch, we had to learn some more rules about something called *recreational games*. Yeah, we always had to learn the rules before we got to play a new game. I sure didn't like to waste a whole lot of time talking about the rules. I just wanted to play.

Counselor Conrad said we needed two volunteers to show us how to play some game they were talking about called *ping-pong*.

Of course, the two big shots who wanted to volunteer were Corrector Cora and Bossy Billy.

Normal Nam came up to me and whispered, "They're going to destroy each other."

Yep, they sure weren't very nice.

"You can't get on the table!" shouted Corrector Cora.

"Hey, Cora," said Bossy Billy, "stop telling me what to do! You're not the boss of me!"

"Oh yeah? Take that!" said Corrector Cora as she slammed the ping-pong ball onto his corner of the table.

He sure looked kind of funny when he swatted the air.

"Looks like you missed!" She laughed real mean.

Boy, did Bossy Billy look surprised.

When it was his turn, he ricocheted the ball off her head.

"No fair!" she shouted. "Foul ball!"

"Wrong game! Wrong rules!" yelled that bossy kid. "We're not playing baseball!"

Then they really started shouting some of the meanest things I'd ever heard.

Yep, Bossy Billy got so mad he looked like he might smash his paddle into the table or throw it clear across the table at Corrector Cora.

But he just shouted instead. "No wonder nobody likes you! You're just a pain-in-the-neck corrector, just like Pip said in his haiku."

"Well," said Corrector Cora, "I sure was happy when that dumb kid, Pip, pushed your head in the mud! You deserved it because you're nothing but a bossy brat!"

Gee, I sure was wishing that they hadn't brought my name into their stupid ol' fight.

Both of our camp counselors had been setting up the horseshoe game, but they stopped what they were doing. Yeah, they came running over to keep those two rotten kids from tearing each other apart.

I was really hoping they'd both get thrown out of summer camp. But they didn't get thrown out. Nope! They just got lectured about something called *bad sportsmanship*.

Yeah, Corrector Cora and Bossy Billy had to run laps for Counselor Becky. So they couldn't play any more games the rest of the day.

Then our camp counselor showed us how to play horseshoes. I thought it was a lot of fun. And I really wasn't too bad at it, except that one of the horseshoes went flying so high it hit the top of the tetherball pole. Boy, did all the kids laugh when it made a big ol' ringing sound.

Counselor Conrad asked me if I'd done that on purpose.

"Hey," I told him, "I probably couldn't hit anything, even if I was aiming at it. Gee, I'm not that good!"

He just shook his head like he knew I was right. "Okay, Pip. I think you've got me there."

Then he gave my shoulder a great big squeeze and said, "You know, today is the first day you didn't get into trouble. In fact, you even proved yourself to be a good teammate for your partner, Nam. Great job, Pip!"

Yeah, I was feeling pretty good. But then he had to go and add, "Don't blow it!"

That sure made me feel kind of bad. I knew I could last another day without causing trouble. Yep! And I was even going to help that shy girl to sing.

When Normal Nam and I got into our bunks that night, we talked about our crazy day.

"I thought Billy and Cora were going to smack each other on the head with their paddles," laughed Nam.

"Me too!" I said. "It sure was the best darn day I've had at this stinking camp!"

Then Normal Nam got kind of quiet. "Don't you like it here?" he asked.

"Well, I guess now I sort of like it. I didn't like it at all before we were bunk buddies. I had to bunk with a whiner, a joker, and a big ol' cheater. There were also a lot of other rotten kids that I'm glad I didn't have to bunk with, like Show-Off Shad, Bossy Billy, and Corrector Cora."

"I know," he said. "Too bad we weren't sharing a room together the whole time."

I felt the same way. Normal Nam was the

nicest kid I'd ever met. So I felt kind of sad when he said that this would be our last night bunking together.

Yeah, before I fell asleep I thought about my day. It was really a pretty great day.

I guess it did make me feel a little bad when Bossy Billy and Corrector Cora were shouting about all the rotten things I'd done to them. But it sure was fun to see them get into trouble for a change. I was just glad it wasn't me for once.

Hey, it's not easy being a kid. And I sure was feeling mixed up. I didn't know why, but I was starting to like camp a little bit. Then I shook my head and wondered what made me think such a strange thing.

9

A Talent Show with Shy Shannon

Normal Nam and I woke up early. We were real excited for our last day at camp. So when the whistle blew, we were the first kids to line up.

Our camp counselor told us, "You will be practicing for your talent show all morning after we eat breakfast." He pulled on his ol' chin hairs. "After lunch you will all need to be ready to perform because your families will be here to watch you." He looked at me and added, "Everyone just do their best!"

After breakfast I found Shy Shannon. She looked kind of sick. I guess she was real nervous.

"Hey, Shannon," I said, "let's just pretend I'm your audience. So look at me. Now try to move your lips to the words in that song."

Shy Shannon hardly moved her mouth at all. Yeah, she was worse than ever.

"Maybe you need to take a shower and practice some more," I told her.

She sort of smiled. "I really wish I could do my part of the talent show in the shower," she said. Then she looked down and added, "Of course I'd use the outside shower and wear my clothes."

Even though she was looking down, I knew her face was real red—yep, sort of like her ears.

That gave me another one of my great ideas. But first I had to look for Counselor Conrad and find out what he thought.

"Hey, Pip, just settle down," he said. "What did you do this time?"

"Uh, nothing." I scratched my head. "At least I don't think I've done anything bad today."

"Well, that's a good start," said Counselor Conrad.

"I just wanted to tell you about my idea to help Shannon sing."

He looked interested, so I told him my idea. When I got done, he just grabbed my shoulder and told me he was real happy that I cared so much about somebody else for a change.

Yeah, I guess I felt pretty good, even if he did have to add "for a change."

I told Shy Shannon that I had to work on something with Counselor Conrad. She looked sort of worried, so I told her just to keep practicing that song and I'd be back soon.

So my camp counselor and I hammered and hammered most of the morning, and Shy Shannon kept listening to that song on Counselor Becky's CD.

Yep, I kept looking inside to see if she was doing any practicing, but she sure wasn't moving her mouth at all. She never even came outside to see what we were doing, but I was glad. It was supposed to be a big surprise.

Counselor Conrad told Counselor Becky what we were doing, and she looked real happy too. Then she said, "I'm going to search the Internet for the sound you'll need."

When the other kids came outside and asked us what we were making, Counselor Conrad told them they'd find out soon enough. Then he told them to get back inside and practice.

I sure did feel kind of special because I was the only one that our camp counselor was helping. I just hoped we'd finish in time for our talent show.

After we put down our hammers, Counselor Conrad said, "You certainly did work hard, Pip." Then he patted me on the back and told me, "I couldn't be more proud of you."

Wow! Nobody had ever told me that they were proud of me before. I didn't even know what to say, but I sure felt real good, even if I was kind of sore from working so hard.

When it was time for lunch, I was so hungry that I ate two big bowls of soup, my sandwich, and half of Nam's sandwich.

"I'm too nervous to eat," said Normal Nam. "But you sure can put it away! Aren't you nervous, Pip?"

"Yeah," I said. "But I've been working kind of hard, so I was real hungry."

"That's right." He looked kind of funny.

"What are you building with Counselor Conrad? Is it some kind of *prop*?"

"What's a prop?" I wanted to know.

He told me, "A prop is an object you use as part of a show. It's like something an actor would use in a movie." Then he smiled real big and said, "Or like a singer might use in a talent show."

Normal Nam sure is good at figuring stuff out. I told him he was right but that it was top secret. He gave me something called a *pinky swear*, so I knew he wouldn't tell anyone.

Then he got kind of quiet and asked, "Hey, Pip, do you think we will get together when summer camp is over?"

"Sure!" I said. "You're my new best friend!"

Yep, Normal Nam wrote his email address on a napkin for me. But I had to tell him that my parents wouldn't let me have my own email. So we wrote down our phone numbers instead.

When we were done, our camp counselors had us all help move our chairs to the other side of the room. They showed us how to take down the tables and move them off to the side.

Then Counselor Conrad told us to go back to our rooms and pack our suitcases because we had to be ready for our families, who would be there soon.

It was real weird, but I'd felt sort of homesick when we'd packed up all our stuff. That didn't make any sense because we weren't even at home. I sure didn't know why I felt kind of sad about leaving summer camp. But I think I did. Yep, just when I was starting to get used to that ol' summer camp, it was time to go.

When we got back to the mess hall, the camp counselors had put up some kind of fancy red curtain that divided the room in half. All of the chairs were facing the curtain.

My stomach was doing flips when I saw some parents start to come in.

I found Shy Shannon biting her fingernails behind the curtain. She sure looked like her stomach was doing flips too.

"Hey, Shannon," I said, "it's not that bad. Who's going to really care anyway?"

"My parents are here," she whispered. "What if I faint?"

"Didn't you ever put on Christmas programs for your parents?" I asked her.

She nodded her head up and down.

"Well, don't you know that our moms and dads like to see us up on a stage? No matter how bad we look or sound, they will always clap for us."

"Yeah, I guess so." She sort of smiled.

I don't know why, but I patted her on the head. And for some reason, I didn't feel so afraid anymore.

When it was finally our turn, I looked under that curtain and saw my family sitting in the front row. Yeah, my mom and dad were there, and so was my big sister, K.D.

Then our camp counselors rolled out the big wooden screen Counselor Conrad and I had built. And Counselor Becky started playing the special rain sound she had on her computer.

Boy, was Shannon ever surprised to see our fake shower. Yep, it sure did look and sound just like a real outside shower.

She was real happy when I told her that she could go behind the screen if she wanted to.

When the music started I pretended to strum the guitar, and then I heard Shannon singing behind the screen. Yeah, she sang even louder than Carole King was singing on the CD. Shy Shannon really did sound good.

Everyone got real quiet, sort of like they couldn't believe what they were hearing.

When I looked over at my mom, she was wiping her eyes like she was crying. But she didn't look sad because she had a gigantic smile on her face.

My dad kept taking a whole bunch of pictures. Yeah, I almost went blind from that darn flash.

Even my sister looked happy. Or maybe she was just smiling because she thought we looked funny. I didn't really know for sure, but I didn't even care.

After we finished, everyone stood up and clapped. Yep, the kids behind the curtain were clapping real hard too.

So I went behind the screen and pulled Shy Shannon out. She was redder than an ol' tomato, but she had the biggest smile I'd ever seen.

When we went back behind the curtain, I told Shy Shannon, "You were great! From now on I'm going to call you 'Showbiz Shannon.'"

She just smiled real big and whispered, "Thanks, Pip. You're not so bad yourself."

Oh yeah, my face sure burned like a furnace.

After all the other kids finished with their songs and dances, we were told to take our parents to the craft room so we could show them our pinecone wreaths and log cabins we'd made.

Of course all of our parents made these weird "oohs" and "ahhs." Then they told us all how special our art projects were.

Only my stinking sister said something mean. "Pip," she said, shaking her head, "those art projects sure are lame."

Yeah, maybe they were kind of goofy, but she sure didn't have to be so rotten. I thought maybe she was a little jealous that I got to go to camp and she didn't.

We got to play those recreational games like ping-pong and horseshoes while our parents stood around yakking.

I was real surprised when I saw Bossy Billy and Corrector Cora playing ping-pong together again.

I heard that ol' corrector start to tell him, "No, no, no, you're doing it all—" But she stopped before she got to her favorite word, *wrong*.

Then Bossy Billy started to say, "Hey, it's my turn to—" but he stopped too and then said, "That's okay, you can take your turn."

Yeah, I was thinking that maybe those two kids really did learn some kind of lesson.

Nam and Shannon both laughed when I threw another horseshoe and it went so high in the air that it hit the top of the tetherball pole again. Boy, I couldn't believe it! Yep, it even made that same loud ringing sound.

When my family met my two new friends, they said how wonderful it was to meet them. Even K.D. was sort of nice.

Then I got to meet Nam's and Shannon's families too.

I sure was shocked when Shannon's mom was so darn friendly and hugged me. She even whispered in my ear, "Thanks for helping my shy girl to finally blossom. I used to be shy too."

Gee, I didn't know people could "blossom." She sure did sound real fancy, sort of like Counselor Becky when she was teaching us poetry.

My very favorite part of all was the giant bonfire we had. We got to roast marshmallows on these real long forks. Of course, the grown-ups kept telling us to "stand back far enough, and don't burn yourselves." They sure do worry a whole lot.

Then the camp counselors showed us all how to make *s'mores*. We had to put our marshmallows between chocolate bars and graham crackers. Yummm! They sure were the best!

When we were all done eating, telling stories, and singing around the campfire, our camp counselors said they had ribbons to pass out to "all of the kids at camp."

Yep, all of the kids got one. Shannon got one for the "Best Singer," and Nam got his for the "Best Speller." Even Billy got one for "Best Tennis Player," and Cora got a ribbon for "Best Haiku."

I sure knew I wouldn't get one because I couldn't do one thing better than anyone else could.

Yeah, I was real surprised when I heard Counselor Conrad call out, "Pip!"

I looked all around. I thought maybe there was another kid named Pip.

But Counselor Conrad gave me a great big wink and said, "Phillip Isaac Penn, this is for you. I'm proud to announce that your ribbon is for the 'Most Improved.' It's very impressive, since this is a brand-new ribbon we made in your honor. You really have proved yourself to be a great team player who has *matured* beyond our expectations."

I really didn't know what the heck he was saying, but I knew it must've been good because even my dad was wiping his eyes and smiling all over his face.

Then my sister said the strangest thing: "Way to go, Pip!" And she even asked my mom and dad if they had camps for kids her age.

Yeah, I was really going to miss that ol' camp.

Sure, it's not very easy being a kid. But there are a whole bunch of fun things we get to do that grown-ups can't do. Yep, I'd still rather be a kid than a mom or a dad, who have to always act so darn *mature.*

Discussion Questions

1. Pip didn't want to go to summer camp. Have you ever had to do something you didn't want to do during your summer vacation? If so, did you end up having fun?

2. Whiner Winston sure complained a lot. How does it make you feel when someone is always complaining? Do you enjoy being around such a person?

3. Joker Joey and Show-Off Shad always wanted to get everyone's attention. Do you think they went about it in the right way? Why or why not?

4. Cheater Chaz was the only character from the first book to make a comeback appearance. Would you do what Pip did, and go along with a cheater, or do you think you'd be able to say no to cheating?

5. Have you ever known someone like Corrector Cora, who seems to enjoy telling people what they are doing wrong? If so, how did that make you feel?

6. Pip made friends with Normal Nam and Shy Shannon. How do you think those two friendships helped Pip to change in the last two chapters?

Acknowledgments

I WOULD LIKE TO ACKNOWLEDGE THE SUPER STAFF AT CEDAR FORT, Inc. who have helped me, such as: Shersta Gatica, the acquisitions editor, who has been so helpful in getting both of my books published; Megan Whittier and Lyle Mortimer, for their great cover design of my first book; Rachel Sharp for her fantastic design on the cover of this book; Melissa Caldwell, for her sharp eye in editing; Mariah Overlock, my last publicist, and Josh Johnson, my current publicist; Donna Selenko; Heidi Doxey; Heather Holm; Emily Showgren; Kirt Forakis; Jennifer Fielding; and all of the other terrific staff members who have helped me on both of my books. A special thanks to Rachel Sharp, who I'm so fortunate to have done these fabulous illustrations for both of my books.

To my loving husband, Brad, and both of my perfect sons, Erik and David, plus Erik's sweet wife, Shawna— I thank them for their support. And to all of my other family members: my wonderful parents, Betty, and Ed and my stepmother, Sherry. My terrific brother Steve, his wife, Diana, and their children, Heather and Tyler—thanks for helping to promote my book. I am so blessed to have sister-in-laws like Diana, Ellie, Sonja, Dee, and Sue, who have come to my book signings and bought my books. I have so many wonderful cousins, especially Kathy, Terry, Karyn, Nancee, and Debbie, who have been such a great support and are like sisters to me. All of my aunts and uncles: Norma, Audrey, Joyce, Phyllis and Bill, and Shirley and Jim, who have been such loyal fans. Thanks also to my friends who have offered encouragement as I've worked on my books—you are treasures to me, each and every one of you, especially my "Sister Chick" Cheryl Casjens. I can't thank you enough for all you have done to help support and promote my books.

A special thanks to my community for their strong support. To Mike and Sue at Mike's Signs, who donated a sign for a local book signing. Much gratitude goes to the Weiser Public Schools, both staff and children, for their continued support. My deep appreciation to Tony, from the Washington County Agriculture Extension Office, for his helpful information on poisonous plants. A huge thanks goes to Delton Walker for his expertise. And I'm very grateful to Pat Hamilton, the Weiser librarian, for being so kind to promote my books with her creative book fairs and book signings.

I have so many people to thank for all of my success, and I hope that everyone knows how much I appreciate them, even if they weren't mentioned by name. I especially want to thank all of my loyal readers who have expressed their delight in reading about my precocious character, Pip. Thanks to all of you, Pip will be able to have more "misadventures" for everyone to enjoy.

About the Author

Donna Peterson has enjoyed writing stories and poetry since she was in the second grade. Donna had her first book, *The Misadventures of Phillip Isaac Penn: It's Not Easy Being a Kid*, published in 2011. She has also been published four times in the *Idaho Magazine* and wrote a weekly humor column, "Kaleidoscope," for the *Three Rivers Chronicle*. Donna recently made a difficult decision to take an early retirement from her job of twelve years with the school district so that she will be able to spend more time doing what she enjoys most: writing for young readers. However, she has signed up on the sub list, so she plans on being involved with school activities.

Donna lives in Idaho with her husband, Brad, and their three beloved pets: Rusty, Sam, and Links. Her son Erik and his lovely wife, Shawna, live in Utah. Her other son, David, just joined them as a roommate while he plans on attending a nearby college in Utah.

Along with writing, Donna's other favorite pastimes include Zumba and photography. Having her first children's book published last year was a dream come true.